Dedicated to all the children of Redding, California. Through their ears I listened to the wind singing through the pines and found the place called Wingsong...A magical place where anything can happen and your dreams come true.

Stephen

If you listen to the wind as it whispers through the pines you will hear a simple, gentle melody. A whispery song about a magical land called Wingsong. If you close your eyes and listen with all your might you can see this magical place.

Wingsong, where everything is real and dreams come true. A place of tall, stately pines and high granite cliffs. A place where butterflies dance. A valley of magic and wonders. Wingsong.

Glitterby Baby

Written by: Stephen Cosgrove
Illustrated by: Robin James

A Serendipity™ Book

PRICE STERN SLOAN
Los Angeles

ISBN: 0-8431-1166-6

Serendipty™ and The Pink Dragon® are trademarks of Price Stern Sloan, Inc.

14 13 12 11 10

As the wind swept through this magic land like a velvet fog it lifted all things to greater heights. From a dried brown leaf to a magnificent butterfly, all things flew higher when they listened to the melodies of Wingsong.

Amidst this majesty of light and lively winds lived a most beautiful little winged horse called Flutterby. She flew on wings that knew all of Wingsong. She soared so high she could touch the sky and then, like an eagle, she would swoop down to tip her wings in the cool crystal pools.

Even with all of this beauty and wonder, Flutterby was lonely. It was hard enough to talk to, let alone understand, butterflies, and beyond those little creatures there was no one. No one to talk to at all.

One day, out of loneliness, Flutterby flew higher than she had ever flown before. Higher than the stately pines and higher than the granite cliffs. Higher and higher until she had flown beyond the magic of Wingsong for the first time in her life. Finally, she was so high that she was in a place where nighttime touches the sky. She gazed about and saw a small isolated meadow far below.

She looked, and looked again. She saw a herd of horses! She dropped like a snowflake swirling quickly to the ground and landed with a gentle click of her heels right in the middle of the herd. They looked at her and she looked at them. For these were not the winged magical creatures of Wingsong, but rather miniature, mortal horses.

The herd was a bit skittish at seeing this winged beauty, and backed away in nervous wonder. Finally, the leader of the herd, a beautiful stallion called Black-Eyed Pete, inched closer and closer until he was nose to nose with Flutterby. With a "whoosh!" and a "snort!" they shared a bonding of breath. Then, as if nothing had happened out of the ordinary, the herd welcomed Flutterby to their meadow and went back to their gentle grazing.

All of the herd, that is, except a beautiful stallion called Black-Eyed Pete and a blushing winged filly called Flutterby.

The stallion, with black mane and tail flying and head held high, would race about the meadow bucking and jumping. For no reason at all he would leap high in the air and kick at a butterfly or reach for the sun. For it could be said that Black-Eyed Pete had fallen head over heels in love with the little grey winged mare.

Flutterby felt the same way. She had never seen anything quite so magnificent as Pete. She would trot about the meadow with her tail held high, her flashing blue eyes following the stallion wherever he went.

The sacred bond and magic of love had united the flying horse Flutterby and the dark stallion Black-Eyed Pete together, forever.

Married by this magical meadow in the bloom of summertime, they spent their time together sharing the tender bits of grass and flowers that grew in great profusion there. Sometimes, in moments of great joy, Flutterby would flutter her wings and soar high in the sky. For the most part, though, she was contented to be near her meadow mate.

As summer wore on Flutterby began to notice that she was gaining weight, but simply thought that she was just eating more and flying less. As fall dropped its leaves and waited for winter's mantle of snow, it became harder and harder for Flutterby to fly at all.

"I have got to lose some weight or I shall never fly again!" she thought to herself. Flutterby would run and run and when she was running as fast as she could she would reach out her wings and try to lift herself off the ground. She would start to soar but then the weight became too much and she would skid across the ground like a leaf caught in a whirlwind.

As she lay there in a tangle of wings and legs she wondered out loud, "Why can't I fly?"

A laughing whinny broke her concentration as an old grey mare helped her to her feet. "It seems, my little Flutterby, that you are going to have a baby. Winged horses who are pregnant can't fly — for their own safety as well as the child's."

Flutterby was overjoyed. "A baby, a child, a foal — what delight!" The old mare continued, "Wait! You will have a hard decision to make. You cannot remain here in a mortal meadow for long after the foal is born. For if you stay you will die."

Saddened by the news of having to leave her beloved Black-Eyed Pete, Flutterby said, "If what is to be is to be then when the child is born we shall fly together back to the magic of Wingsong."

"Ahhh!" said the old mare. "There are two sides to every coin. Because Pete is mortal and you are magic, the child may or may not be able to fly. If it is able then it may fly away with you. If not, the child must stay here in the mortal meadow."

Flutterby wandered and waited, wishing for her child to be born with strong wings.

In springtime, Flutterby foaled in a burst of starlight — the child was born. As the sun sparkled across this meadow of mortals it splashed upon a resting Flutterby, a proud stallion called Black-Eyed Pete and a gangly little filly they called Glitterby Baby.

Flutterby looked over the flanks of the tiny foal and saw wings that were very, very small. Heartened by hope and desire she thought quietly to herself, "The wings will grow in time. They must! They must!"

Glitterby grew, but with each day Flutterby became sadder and sadder; the wings didn't seem to be any bigger. But the baby was healthy and strong and would gallop on wobbly legs about the meadow, chasing shadows in the wind.

One day as the child lay sleeping, Flutterby unfurled her wings and lifted up into the sky. It felt so good to fly again, to feel the cool breezes brush her mane. Her reverie was short-lived, for suddenly she heard a terrified scream from below. She swooped down beside the startled foal, who had become frightened when her mother flew away.

Flutterby soothed the tiny horse with a gentle nuzzle of her nose, and the words of the old grey mare echoed in her mind, "If the baby cannot fly, she must stay here in the mortal meadow, and you must go to Wingsong alone!"

One day the entire herd gathered in the middle of the meadow with Flutterby, Glitterby and Pete. "It is time," said the old mare, "to see if Glitterby can fly."

With a bit of coaching from her mother, the little filly galloped to the other end of the meadow. Then, with a flick of her tail, she ran as fast as she could to the center of the meadow and tried to fly. She leaped high into the air, but she did not fly. Instead, she skidded in a heap right in the middle of the herd. Flutterby helped her to her feet and off she went to try again, and again. But no matter how hard she tried, she could not fly. Flutterby knew she would have to leave the child with her father, Black-Eyed Pete.

With tears streaming from her eyes, she nuzzled Glitterby and told her that she must stay with the herd in the mortal meadow. The little foal could do nothing but cry as she stood in the shadow of her father. Flutterby knew that the longer she put it off, the harder it would be, so she spread her wings and leaped for the sky.

The little foal, Glitterby, ran around and around the herd shouting, "Mother, don't leave! Mother, don't leave!" It was to no avail. Flutterby flew higher and higher into the sky, blinded by the tears in her eyes.

She was nearly as high as where the night touches the sky, but she could still hear Glitterby neighing below. It seemed that she could almost hear more clearly as she flew higher. She looked down for one final glimpse of Glitterby before she had to leave for Wingsong forever.

There, between a cloud and the meadow, she could see a small bird madly flapping its wings in the wind. She looked again, and then again. It was not a bird she saw, but a little winged horse called Glitterby Baby determinedly flying with all her might to catch her mother and take her rightful place in the sky.

Far below, a beautiful stallion called Black-Eyed Pete sadly walked back to the meadow. Sad, but happy for Glitterby, who was where she wanted to be.

AS WE LOOK AROUND US
AT OUR MORTAL SIDE AND SIGH
REMEMBER A PLACE CALLED
WINGSONG
THEN, LIFT YOUR WINGS AND FLY

Serendipity Books

Written by Stephen Cosgrove
Illustrated by Robin James

Enjoy all the delightful books in the Serendipity Series:

BANGALEE	LEO THE LOP TAIL THREE
BUTTERMILK	LITTLE MOUSE ON THE PRAIRIE
BUTTERMILK BEAR	MAUI-MAUI
CATUNDRA	MEMILY
CRABBY GABBY	MING LING
CREOLE	MINIKIN
CRICKLE-CRACK	MISTY MORGAN
DRAGOLIN	MORGAN AND ME
THE DREAM TREE	MORGAN AND YEW
FANNY	MORGAN MINE
FEATHER FIN	MORGAN MORNING
FLUTTERBY	THE MUFFIN MUNCHER
FLUTTERBY FLY	MUMKIN
FRAZZLE	NITTER PITTER
GABBY	PERSNICKITY
GLITTERBY BABY	PISH POSH
THE GNOME FROM NOME	POPPYSEED
GRAMPA-LOP	RAZ-MA-TAZ
THE GRUMPLING	RHUBARB
HUCKLEBUG	SASSAFRAS
JALOPY	SERENDIPITY
JINGLE BEAR	SNIFFLES
KARTUSCH	SQUABBLES
KIYOMI	SQUEAKERS
LADY ROSE	TICKLE'S TALE
LEO THE LOP	TRAPPER
LEO THE LOP TAIL TWO	WHEEDLE ON THE NEEDLE
ZIPPITY ZOOM	

The above books, and many others, can be bought wherever books are sold, or may be ordered directly from the publisher.

PRICE STERN SLOAN
Los Angeles